A Comic by Cooner!

Characters, story, and artwork by John Nunnemacher

My Bigger Boyfriend, Volume Two, released December 2025 by FurPlanet Productions.
Print ISBN: 978-1-61450-680-5

Contact information: Email at **cooner@cooner.art** • On the web at **toonraccoon.art** or **linktr.ee/cooner**
Publisher on the web: **furplanet.com**

Table of Contents

Foreword

What a piece of joy you hold in your hands.

The joy of genuine love, the joy of friendship and community.

The joy of a boyfriend whose damn titties are bigger than your head.

I met John back when we were practically neighbors out in San Jose, CA. We had both done work for the local furry convention and became quick friends. One day in the fall of 2016, I was about to leave San Jose for Vancouver to work in the animation industry. John and I went out for cheesesteaks and talked shop. Trust me when I say, the warmth and joy from these pages can be traced directly back to their own author.

Two major historical events later, *My Bigger Boyfriend* was born.

Not to brag, but I'm somewhat of a homoqueer myself. I live in a gay city and love a bigger homoqueer than me. I see the characters in *My Bigger Boyfriend* every day—trans men, big women, lovable meathead dingdongs named Chad—they're all a part of our rainbow. *My Bigger Boyfriend* is a capsule of an affectionate look at queer sexuality, regulars in our favorite bar, the domesticity of purchasing new couches, working a job you didn't expect because it keeps you fed. This is the day to day life between making history and fighting for our rights.

So get comfortable on them couch cushion-sized pecs you have available (if you're lucky) and enjoy.

—Grey "BAPHYPAWS" White
November 2025

Introduction

Why do I do this?

I think many readers of my comics will agree that the world, especially in the United States, has gotten materially worse since the first print volume of *My Bigger Boyfriend* was published only a couple years ago. It feels like governments, business service corporations and internet service platforms are growing increasingly hostile to queer, trans, sex-positive, and even furry creators and audiences. Attacks on immigrants and BIPOC by quasi-paramilitary government agents are almost unprecedented in the modern era. And as a backdrop, the abandonment of green initiatives and the coercion of generative artificial intelligence pushes our economy and our environment to the very brink.

Dark times indeed.

◆

When I first started developing *My Bigger Boyfriend,* I had one very important precept in mind: to champion openness, diversity, and

Lance Lion says Trans Lives Matter.

acceptance in my little world. My two main characters, Pride and Ocean, were gay, of course; but I wanted to expand the options well beyond that. Setting the story in a queer part of town and positioning Pride's job working at a gay bar, I was able to populate the cast with trans characters, bisexual characters, nonbinary characters. Characters in committed relationships, and characters more open in their explorations. Characters of non-traditional beauty. And yes, even a few straight characters and relationships here and there.

And I wanted to portray everyone living and working side-by-side with no discrimination and no judgement. There are no major "coming out" arcs, no conflicts arising from religious or cultural bigotry. Those kinds of stories are important, of course … expressing people's lived experiencing, and warning of the harm that comes from such societal prejudice. But my goal was to demonstrate an island of respite from those issues, a vision of what the world can look like if everyone works together.

Of course, LGBTQ+ prejudice is far from the only prejudice in our world.

As I started moving into a story arc where the 24-hour Taco Hut that Pride and Ocean frequent became more of a focal point, I decided that the people running such a business should be Mexican immigrants, and should be portrayed with the same respect I try to use for all my queer characters. And so arose the blended Taco Hut family including Pepe Polar Bear; his abuela, Alma Águila; and their employee Carlos Cuervo.

In keeping with my priorities, I wanted the characters to speak naturally, with the bilingual mixing of English and Spanish words I've seen not only in media, but also among my own friends. Sadly, I had made the fatal decision decades ago in middle school to choose German for my language study requirement. As a result I speak zero to little Spanish. The last thing I wanted to do was pepper their dialog with cartoonish ejaculations of *"¡Si!"* and *"¡Madre de Dios!"* and call it a day.

As luck would have it, I'd recently come in contact with a fellow named Corvus Cantum, a translator from Mexico who is a long-time fan of *My Bigger Boyfriend*, who offered his services. For every strip featuring those characters, I would send him an early copy of the script written entirely in English; he would choose particular phrases and expressions to translate into Spanish. He would also suggest cultural details and colloquialisms to

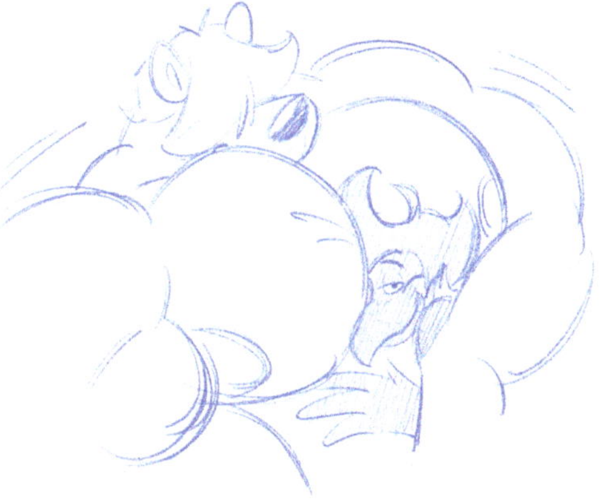

Quick doodle of Corvus Cantum,
Ocean Otter's biggest fan

incorporate into the story. He even managed to differentiate a few different dialects the various characters would be speaking in.

As far as I'm concerned, by helping to incorporate a bit of authenticity into my multicultural, multilingual cast, Corvus has immensely expanded the breath and depth of the *My Bigger Boyfriend* world.[1]

Corvus Cantum, drawn by Alen @alexxxnttt.bsky.social, vs. Carlos Cuervo at Taco Hut. Separated at birth …?

◆ ◆ ◆

It is disappointing and distressing that even as I was writing and portraying the Taco Hut family and the rest of my queer cast, forces were at work causing us to rapidly descend to the point we're at as I write this text in late 2025.

I can't lie and say this hasn't been a difficult year for me. A lot of my creative plans got derailed; it's been difficult to stay focused on long-term projects when I don't know what the state the world will be in the

---

[1] You can find Corvus on FurAffinity at https://www.furaffinity.net/user/vfd13, or on Bluesky at https://bsky.app/profile/corvuscantum.bsky.social.

coming months or years. (Eagle-eyed readers may notice a long production gap where the publication dates jump from February to August 2025. I just wasn't able to focus on the comic for that length of time.)

Yet, I must carry on. When there is pain, sadness, and oppression in the world, that must be countered with joy and resistance. When the technocratic class wants to beat everyone into submission, joy is resistance, as the adage goes.

The last thing I wanted to do at this stage of my life was to be writing political diatribes. But art is necessarily political, so here we are. As a reader of queer comics, if you would like to see queer and diverse comics and stories survive and thrive, I would ask you to please consider doing a few things in the coming year.

- Do what you can to help at-risk communities: LGBTQ+, BIPOC, immigrants, those in poverty. Vote for candidates and initiatives that will best help them. Listen when they speak. Donate to their (vetted) causes if you can afford to do so. Intervene on their behalf to protect them if or when you can. Each of us has different talents or resources we can execute, but all of us can play our part, however small it seems.

- Support queer, BIPOC, and independent creators in general. Buy their books or merchandise, join their Patreons, support their campaigns, repost and help spread the word when they're promoting their creations. We need them telling the stories and making the art that corporate media will never do, and we need their voices now more than ever. (And thanks for buying this book!)

• Pay attention and do what you can in pressuring payment processors like Mastercard and Paypal to stop discriminating against and de-banking creators and publishers of queer, adult, and sex-positive content. Fight to prevent governments and internet companies from censoring or banning queer, adult, sex-positive content under the false pretense of "protecting the children." Make calls, send letters, whatever you can do.

• Reject government and corporate surveillance, and reject generative A.I. It may seem like fun, but it destroys the environment with its energy use, and it rapidly erodes your personal capacity to think and perform even menial tasks on your own. And at scale, it's a tool for technocrats to silence voices and steal income to enhance their own power and profits.

◆ ◆ ◆

So, why do I do this? Ultimately, this is why. In all other aspects I try to vote or donate or contribute as much as I can. But I feel the thing I'm best at, maybe the only thing I'm good at, is creating silly stories and silly characters and silly worlds for them to play in.

So I'll keep on writing *My Bigger Boyfriend,* keep developing *Coyena Comics* and various other projects, for as long as there is breath in my lungs and power in my tablet and as long as I can hold a pencil in my hand. I certainly hope that you, dear readers, enjoy them, and that together we can keep alive the dream of a happier, more fair, more equitable world.

And someday, together, we will manifest that world into reality.

—Cooner
November 2025

Insets: Artwork for a set of pin-on buttons produced in November 2022.

My Bigger Boyfriend

Volume Two:
December 14, 2022 through November 12, 2025

I DUNNO HOW YOU PUT UP WITH ME, PRIDE.
I WAS A SMALL CLUMSY OAF BEFORE AND NOW I'LL BE A BIG CLUMSY OAF FOREVER!
©COONER · 12/14/2022

EVEN NOW, WITH ALL THESE BIG STRONG MUSCLES--

EVEN WITH THESE BROAD PECS--
--AND THESE BULGING BICEPS, THESE RIPPLING ABDOMINALS--

HOW CAN YOU STILL LOVE ME LIKE THIS??
HNNNG
HUFF

HUNNY! YOU KNOW I LOVE YOU FOR YOU!
WE'VE HAD CHALLENGES, SURE--

BUT WE'RE HERE TO HELP EACH OTHER, NO MATTER WHAT, RIGHT?
I GUESS--

©COONER 12/28/2022

BUT ALSO, I'M KINDA HOT NOW, RIGHT?
WELL, CLEARLY, DUH.

CHEER UP, HUNNY. ARE YOU STILL HUNGRY?
NAWWW. NOT REALLY ANYMORE.

YOU SURE? WE CAN STOP BY TACO HUT!
I DUNNO--

RRRUMBLE

I THINK YOU NEED TACOS.
BETRAYED BY MINE OWN BODY--
©COONER 1/4/2023

Strip #114

TACO HUT

IT'S *LATE*. IT'LL PROBABLY JUST BE *PEPE* WORKING.
©COONER 1/11/2023

¡BIENVENIDOS! ¡BUENAS NOCHES!

OH, IT'S *YOU* MUCHACHOS!
GOOD THING WE JUST HAD OUR *DELIVERY TRUCK* IN EARLIER TONIGHT!

AT PRIDE & OCEAN'S FAVORITE LATE-NIGHT FOOD STAND...
TACO HUT

¿QUE VAN A QUERER LOS NOVIOS?*
HMMM--
©COONER 1/18/2023
*"WHAT WILL THE BOYFRIENDS WANT TONIGHT?"

I THINK I'LL JUST GET MY REGULAR ORDER TONIGHT!
YEAH?

--AND ONE GRUB CHALUPA, PLEASE!
YEAH! ONE TICK AND BLUEBERRY STREET TACO--

¡MUY BIEN! AND FOR YOU, JOVEN?
HM, I'M NOT VERY HUNGRY TONIGHT.
TAP
TAP

I GUESS JUST THREE SALMON AND SEAWEED TACOS--
--AND THREE SEARED TUNA TACOS.

AND A MONSTER CHICKEN BURRITO, DOUBLE MEAT. AND ORDER OF BEEF TAQUITOS.
AND TWO HALIBUT TACOS WITH A SIDE OF HOT SEAWEED SALSA.
©COONER 1/25/2023

OH! AND FIVE TAMARIND TILAPIA TACOS.
AND A LARGE ORDER OF CHIPS AND GUACAMOLE--
TAP
TAP

--AND A TWELVE-PACK OF TINY TACOS--
--TWO MORE TUNA TACOS, AND THREE YELLOWTAIL TACOS--
-TAP-
-TAP-
-TAP-

AND AN EXTRA-LARGE HORCHATA, POR FAVOR!
-TAP-

©COONER 2/1/2023

IS THAT ALL, JOVEN--?
YOU'VE ORDERED WAY MORE THAN THAT YOUR LAST FEW TIMES HERE!

PUES, ¡NO ME SOPRENDE!
YOU MUST BE ON A DIRTY BULKING CYCLE, WITH ALL THE MASS YOU'VE BEEN PACKING ON!

HAHA, YEAH, SORTA, I GUESS.
BUT -- GOTTA WATCH PENNIES, Y'KNOW. WHAT WITH LOSING MY JOB AND ALL.

¡AH CHINGA! OCEAN, YOU LOST ANOTHER JOB?
YEAH.

HMMMMMMM.
WHAT SIZE JACKET DO YOU WEAR?
©COONER 2/8/2023

I HAD THIS SPECIAL MADE A COUPLE YEARS AGO, FOR MYSELF.
BUT I'VE BEEN SO BUSY RUNNING THE SHOP, I HAVEN'T HAD TIME TO USE IT.

IF IT FITS, THE JOB IS YOURS IF YOU WANT IT, MUCHACHO --

¡AH, PERFECTO! HERE IT IS--!

BEST TACOS IN WEST QUEERTON!
©COONER 2/15/2023

WHERE'S THE BEEF TAQUITOS? HERE!
©COONER 2/22/2023

PEPE! THANK YOU FOR OFFERING OCEAN A JOB! ARE YOU SURE ABOUT THIS?
¡SÍ! HE'S SURE TO GRAB ATTENTION AND BRING MORE CLIENTES!

BESIDES, THE JOB COMES WITH A 50% DISCOUNT ON FOOD!

ARE YOU SURE YOU CAN AFFORD THAT, IN OCEAN'S CASE?
CIERTO—LET'S MAKE IT 10%.

HONEY, YOU GOT A *NEW JOB!* I'M SO *PROUD* OF YOU!
PEPE SAYS I CAN START MY FIRST FULL SHIFT *TOMORROW!*

IT WAS AWFUL NICE OF HIM TO GIVE ME A *STARTING BONUS,* TOO!
©COONER 3/1/2023

YOU DIDN'T SPEND IT ALL ON *TACOS* ALREADY, DID YOU?
HECK NO! I HAD *ENOUGH* TO EAT TONIGHT!

I JUST GRABBED A *TACO 12-PACK* FOR *LATER.*

MAYBE YOU CAN PAD YOUR SAVINGS ACCOUNT WITH THE REST!
UMM, PRIDE— I HAVE A LITTLE CONFESSION TO MAKE.

I'M AFRAID I— I BROKE THE SOFA THIS MORNING.*
AFTER YOU LEFT FOR WORK.
©COONER 3/8/2023
*-STRIP #36!

AWWW, HUNNY—
NOW THAT I HAVE A JOB IT'S ONLY FAIR WE MAKE ONE MORE STOP ON THE WAY HOME.

24 HOUR SOFA MART
BUY NINE SOFAS GET THE 10TH FOR $1

AT THE ALL-NITE SOFA STORE ...
HOW LONG HAVE WE HAD THAT OLD HAND-ME-DOWN COUCH FROM MY DAD?
24 HOUR SOFA MART
BUY NINE SOFAS GET THE 10TH FOR $1

HMM, A FEW YEARS AT LEAST?
OH, GOSH, HUNNY! DO YOU REALIZE THIS WILL BE OUR FIRST BIG FURNITURE PURCHASE TOGETHER?

OMG! OMG! OMG!
OMG! OMG! OMG!

I FEEL SO — DOMESTICATED!
YEAH!!
©COONER 3/22/2023

APOLOGIES FOR INTERRUPTING YOUR REVELRY, GENTLEMEN. MAY I HELP YOU?
OH, SORRY!

CAN WE BUY A NEW SOFA PLEASE?

©COONER 3/29/2023

SIR, THIS IS "SOFA-MART."

OF COURSE! WE HAVE THE LARGEST SELECTION OF SOFAS IN THE TRI-STATE AREA.

MAY I ASK WHAT BUDGET YOU'RE WORKING WITH?
ABSOLUTELY!

WE CAN GO UP TO ABOUT $300!
©COONER 4/5/2023

ALLOW ME TO SHOW YOU TO OUR POPULAR "FRATERNITY FLOPHOUSE" MODELS, THIS WAY.

"FRATERNITY FLOPHOUSE" IS OUR MOST ECONOMICAL MODEL.
AVAILABLE IN PINK, AQUA, OR PUCE.
WOULD YOU CARE TO TRY IT OUT?
©COONER 4/12/2023

OCEAN, HUNNY—?

I FEEL LIKE THAT WOULD BE A REALLY BAD IDEA.

OH MAN—THAT SOFA ISN'T GONNA CUT IT, AND I CAN'T AFFORD ANYTHING BETTER!
DON'T WORRY, HUNNY! WHAT IF WE DO THIS—

THE STORE OFFERS PAYMENT PLANS. USE YOUR MONEY FOR A DOWN PAYMENT—
THEN WE'LL PAY THE REST OFF OVER SIX MONTHS!

OH MY GOSH, PRIDE – DO YOU REALIZE–?
YES–!
©COONER 4/19/2023

OUR FIRST CREDIT DEBT TOGETHER!!

THIS IS THE *OTTERMAN TUSHMASTER 6000.*
TITANIUM STEEL FRAME RATED TO *1,800 POUNDS.*
ADAPTABLE *MICRO-FOAM CUSHIONING* FOR THE *UTMOST* IN COMFORT.

THREE DIFFERENT RECLINING ZONES WITH BUILT-IN *LEG RESTS.*
HEIGHT-ADJUSTABLE SEATS AT THE TOUCH OF A *BUTTON.*

BUILT-IN *REMOTE CONTROL CADDY.*
AND ALTERNATELY *HEATED* OR *CHILLED* ARM REST *CUP HOLDERS* TO KEEP BEVERAGES *WARM* OR *COLD.*
©COONER 4/26/2023

HUNNY?
OCEAN, I THINK I'M IN *LOVE!*

GENTLEMEN, YOU HAVE MADE AN *EXCELLENT* CHOICE.
THIS SOFA WILL GIVE YOU *YEARS* OF *COMFORT*.

NOW. OUR *DELIVERY* OPTIONS START AT *$100—*
OH, WE DON'T *NEED* DELIVERY!

SIR. YOU *NEED* DELIVERY FOR SOMETHING AS *BIG* AS A SOFA.
HONESTLY WE DON'T!

©COONER 5/10/2023

Strip #130

NOW *THERE'S* SOMETHING YOU DON'T SEE EVERY DAY, *CHAUNCEY.*
WHAT'S *THAT,* EDGAR?
BUS STOP
©COONER 5/17/2023

A *PURPLE* OTTERMAN TUSHMASTER 6000.
BUS STOP

QUEERTON MANOR
620
60-69

WELL, THERE IT IS! I MUST SAY IT REALLY DOES TIE THE ROOM TOGETHER.
YUP!

MIND IF I TRY IT OUT?
©COONER 5/24/2023

WE JUST WENT INTO DEBT FOR FIVE YEARS FOR THIS!
MIGHT AS WELL!

Strip #132

PRIIIDE!

PRIIIIDE!
OOOH PRIIIIDE!

PRIDE?
YOU HAVE GOT TO TRY THIS THING!
©COONER 6/7/2023

OKAY. I AM GONNA TRY TO BE *REAL CAREFUL* HERE.

CREAK
©COONER 6/21/2023

RIGHT?!

I--I *THINK* THIS WILL BE OKAY!

HONEY! WE HAVE A *SOFA* AGAIN!

MMM, THIS IS A *VERY* COMFY COUCH.
©COONER 7/5/2023

YOU KNOW WHAT *I* THINK WE SHOULD DO, HUNNY?
WHAT'S THAT?

I THINK WE SHOULD *"BREAK IN"* THIS SOFA.

MMMF! IT *HAS* BEEN A FEW *HOURS*--

QUEERTON MANOR
620
60-69
THUMP
THUMP
THUMP

MMMM, I LOVE YOU SO MUCH. AND YOUR NEW SIZE IS REALLY GROWING ON ME.
YEAH--

I'M JUST REALLY GLAD WE CAN STILL-- DO STUFF.
OH, TISH-TOSH, HUNNY--

YOU KNOW WE'LL ALWAYS FIT, NO MATTER WHAT!
©COONER 7/12/2023

THIS NEW SOFA IS SO COMFY.

YEAH. NOW I KINDA WISH OUR BED WAS THIS COMFORTABLE!
SPEAKING OF THAT--

WE SHOULD REALLY THINK ABOUT GETTING A BIGGER BED SOMETIME SOON.
©COONER 7/19/2023

HMM. WE SHOULD MAYBE THINK ABOUT GETTING A BIGGER BEDROOM.

OOOOH, THE *SUN'S* COMING UP!
WE'LL *BOTH* NEED TO GET TO *WORK* IN A FEW HOURS!

WE'VE BEEN UP *ALL NIGHT LONG*-- BUT IT'S BEEN SUCH A *WILD, CRAZY* EVENING!
I'M STILL WIDE *AWAKE!* YOU?

YEAH, *SAME!*
THERE'S NO *WAY* I COULD FALL ASLEEP ANYTIME SOON!
©COONER 8/2/2023

ZZZZZZZZZZZZZZZZZZZZZZZZZZZZZZZZZZZ
ZZZZZZZZZZZZZZZZZZZZZZZZZZZZZZZZZ
ZZZZZZZZZZZZZZZZZZZZZZZZZZZZZZZZZZ

LATER THAT MORNING, AT THE LAVENDER LION...
MORNIN', BOSS! YOU'RE IN EARLY!
YEAH, THE BOYS WERE IN THIS MORNING TO INSTALL THE NEW BARTOP.*
AND AFTER LAST NIGHT I WANTED TO GO OVER THE BOOKS AGAIN.
*-STRIP #109!

I'M DONE WITH ARM WRESTLING, BUT I GOT TO THINKING--
THERE'S MORE WE COULD DO TO BOOST ATTENDANCE AND SALES.
©COONER 8/9/2023

OOH! LIKE STAGING A BURLESQUE SHOW?!
HMM -- SOMETHING LIKE THAT.

WELL, I DO HAVE SOME THOUGHTS.
I WAS HOPING PRIDE WOULD BE IN EARLY TO BOUNCE IDEAS.
©COONER 8/16/2023

I'LL GIVE HIM A CALL IF YOU WANT!
SURE, DEAR.

THOUGH I WOULDN'T BE SURPRISED IF HE HAD A LATE NIGHT.
OH?

I MEAN! IF I WAS GOING HOME WITH A HANDSOME HUNK LIKE OCEAN--!

I TRIED TO BE LIKE GRACE KELLY... BUT ALL HER LOOKS WERE TOO SAD ...
©COONER 8/23/2023

:GROAN: HULLO?

OH MY! PRIDE--
DID YOU HIT THE CAMERA BUTTON BY MISTAKE?!

--ACK!!
NOW THAT'S A VIEW I'D LOVE TO WAKE UP TO!

LATE NIGHT? I MEAN, AFTER LEAVING THE BAR?
OH YEAH.
©COONER 8/30/2023

WE STOPPED FOR TACOS--
AND ENDED UP AT SOFA MART BUYING A NEW COUCH.

MM-HMM! I SEE!
YEAH.

FOLLOWED, OF COURSE, BY NEKKID TIME!

Strip #144

ANYWAY, LANCE ASKED IF YOU COULD COME IN A BIT EARLY.
HE WANTED TO TALK SOME EVENT PLANNING WITH YOU.
SURE SURE. I'M UP NOW, I'LL BE IN SOON.
©COONER 9/6/2023

ALRIGHT, I'LL LET HIM KNOW! SEE YOU HERE!
YEAH I'M UP.

I'M UP.

ZZZZZZZZZZZZZZZZZZZZZZZZZ
ZZZZZZZZZZZZZZZZZZZZZZZZ
ZZZZZZZZZZZZZZZZZZZZZZ
ZZZZZZZZZZZZZZZZZZZZZ
ZZZ

PRIDE!! HUNNY!!
WE BETTER GET UP SOON!

OH CRAP! I GOTTA GET IN TO MEET LANCE!
YEAH, AND I GOTTA GET TO TACO HUT.
©COONER 9/13/2023

QUICK CHANGE OF CLOTHES AND I'M OUTTA HERE--
YEAH, SAME--

QUEERTON MANOR
620
60-69
THUMP
THUMP
THUMP

Strip #146

PHEW! MADE IT! WITH MINUTES TO SPARE!
I WAS AFRAID WE'D BE LATE.

OH YEAH? I WASN'T TOO WORRIED!
YOU WEREN'T?

NAW. I THINK YOU BROKE SEVERAL WORLD SPEED RECORDS BEFORE WE LEFT THE HOUSE!

I -- GUESS AT SOME POINT WE'LL HAVE TO THINK ABOUT ANOTHER CAR.
-- OH YEAH!
BUS STOP

I ALWAYS WANTED ONE OF THOSE COOL SPORTY LITTLE TWO-SEATER MIATAS!
BUS STOP

BUS STOP

ORRR -- MAYBE SOMETHING A LITTLE BIGGER AND MORE UTILITARIAN.
BUS STOP
RCOONER 10/04/2023

Strip #148

HERE IT IS! IT'S NICE WE CAN *BOTH* TAKE THE SAME *BUS LINE* INTO TOWN!
DOWNTOWN
069
420

GOOD *MORNING,* MS. BUS DRIVER!
DOWNTOWN
069
420

DOWNTOWN
069
420
©COONER 10/11/2023

ERM. I THINK MAYBE I'D BETTER *WALK* INTO TOWN.
DOWNTOWN
069
420

AWW, MAN.
I COULDN'T EVEN FIT ON THE BUS.
WE'RE GONNA HAVE TO BUY A NEW CAR.

I BROKE OUR COUCH. I BROKE THE BEDROOM DOOR. I BROKE LANCE'S BARTOP.
I CAN'T FIT MOST OF MY CLOTHES.
AND MY APPETITE IS COSTING US A SMALL FORTUNE.
©COONER 10/18/2023

THIS NEW SIZE IS REALLY CAUSING A LOT OF EXPENSE AND INCONVENIENCE.

AND I AM WEIRDLY TURNED ON BY THAT!

MEANWHILE ... AT THE LAVENDER LION ...
ISSS PRIDE WORKING AGAIN TODAY?
HE SHOULD BE ON HIS WAY IN.

SSSPLENDID! I'M NOT SSSURPRISSSED IF HE'SSS RUNNING LATE AFTER LASSST NIGHT!
INDEED. IT WAS QUITE A SPECTACLE.

AND THAT OTTER! WHAT A SSSTRAPPING SSSPECIMEN! I WOULDN'T MIND SSSEEING MORE OF HIM AROUND THESSSE PARTSSS!
ERR, YEAH.
©COONER 10/25/2023

OH! I JUSSST NOTICCCED, ISSS THISSS A NEW BARTOP?

OH! HERE'S THE PHONECALL I WAS WAITING FOR.
IF YOU NEED ANYTHING, CHAD CAN COVER UNTIL PRIDE GETS HERE.
SSSURE THING!
©COONER 11/1/2023

HEY, SANDY.
SSSALUTATIONSSS, MY DEAR CHAD!

DID I HEAR YOU DISCUSSING--
--BICEPS AND PECS AND SUCH?
OH YESSS! THEY ARE VERY ENTICCCING!

I REALLY HOPE OCCCEAN COMESSS AROUND MORE OFTEN TO SSSHOW THEM OFF!

CORIE! SORRY I'M RUNNING A BIT LATE.
OH, S'OKAY! LANCE IS TAKING A CALL IN HIS OFFICE, HE'LL BE OUT SOON.

SSSSSSOOOOO, YOUR BOYFRIEND -- HE MUST BE ON ONE HECK OF A WORKOUT ROUTINE!
HE'S PACKING ON MUSCLE LIKE CRAZY!
©COONER 11/8/2023

HEH -- YEAH, SOMETHING LIKE THAT!
WELL, HE LOOKS GREAT! AND -- IF YOU DON'T MIND MY WONDERING --

HE ALSO LOOKS LIKE HE'S PACKING ONE HELL OF A SUMMER BEEF SAUSAGE IN THERE!

CORIE! I DIDN'T KNOW YOU WERE INTO HUGE MUSCLE GUYS.
OH, YOU KNOW ME!

BIG OR SMALL, BOY OR GIRL, ANYTHING INBETWEEN --
I APPRECIATE THE BEAUTY OF THE ANIMAL FORM IN ALL ITS DIVERSITY!
©COONER 11/15/2023

BUT I'LL ADMIT, AS A PLUS-SIZED GAL, IT'S NOT OFTEN I SEE SOMEONE LARGER THAN ME!
HMM, I NEVER THOUGHT ABOUT THAT!

CONFIDENTIALLY, SOMEONE OCEAN'S SIZE COULD WRESTLE ME TO THE GROUND ANY DAY!
TMI!! TMI!!

HEY *PRIDE?* CAN YOU, UHH, *TALK* FOR A MINUTE?
OF *COURSE*, CHAD! WHAT'S *UP?*
©COONER 11/22/2023

TH-*THANKS* FOR HOW YOU *HANDLED* THINGS LAST NIGHT. I-IT WAS ACTUALLY PRETTY *GRACIOUS* OF YOU.
OH? SURE!

YEAH. AND *AFTERWARDS,* I GOT TO *HOOK UP* WITH THAT HYENA, *HAYLIE!*
OH, YEAH? THAT'S *GREAT,* CHAD!

HELL YEAH! WE *BONED* IN THE *BROOM CLOSET* RIGHT THERE!
TMI!! TMI!!

ALSO -- I WANTED TO APOLOGIZE TO YOU, PRIDE.
OH?

YEAH. I'VE BEEN TRYING TO GET YOU TO SLEEP WITH ME FOR MONTHS.
WHEN IT SHOULD HAVE BEEN OBVIOUS THAT YOU WEREN'T INTERESTED.
©COONER 11/29/2023

SO, I'M SORRY --
THANK YOU, CHAD! I REALLY APPRECIATE THAT!

I'M SORRY THAT YOU NEVER GOT THE CHANCE TO SHACK UP WITH THIS BODY!!

GOOD MORNING. EVERYONE BEHAVING TODAY?
OH YES, FOR SURE, LANCE!

YES, WE'RE ALL GOOD NOW, BOSS!
AND I'VE REALLY SELF-ACTUALIZED AND TRULY LEARNED SOMETHING ABOUT MYSELF.

DON'T LAY IT ON TOO THICK, CHAD.
NO, BOSS, REALLY!
©COONER 12/6/2023

I LEARNED THAT I REALLY DIG HYENA CHICKS!

WELL, THAT'S JUST SWELL.
CHAD, MIND THINGS HERE FOR A BIT LONGER? I NEED TO TALK TO PRIDE IN MY OFFICE.

SURE THING, BOSS!
GREAT. THIS SHOULD ONLY TAKE A FEW MINUTES.

OH, BY THE WAY, PRIDE?
YEAH, CHAD?
©COONER 1/17/2024

IF YOU DO EVER CHANGE YOUR MIND -- MY OFFER STILL STANDS!

LANCE, BEFORE WE START -- AGAIN, WE'RE SORRY ABOUT THE BARTOP.*
DON'T MENTION IT. WATER UNDER THE BRIDGE.
*-STRIP #109!

NO, WAIT -- ONE MOMENT.
©COONER 1/24/2024

AUUUGH-WHYYYYYY!?! WAAH-HAHA-HAH...

OKAY. NOW IT'S WATER UNDER THE BRIDGE.

ANYWAY.
MUCH AS I HATE TO *ADMIT* IT, OCEAN AND CHAD'S LITTLE *PERFORMANCE* LAST NIGHT WAS A *BOON* FOR BUSINESS.

IT'S MADE ME CONSIDER THAT PERHAPS WE SHOULD BE PLANNING MORE *EVENTS* HERE AT THE *LAVENDER LION.*

SO, I *JUST* GOT OFF THE PHONE WITH MY *HUSBAND.*

WAIT -- LANCE, YOU HAVE A HUSBAND?!
©COONER 1/31/2024

HAHA. I'M JUST JOKING, OF COURSE. HOW IS SAL DOING?
HE'S BEEN REALLY BUSY WITH WORK AND TRAVEL.

NO DOUBT! I FEEL LIKE I HAVEN'T SEEN HIM IN MONTHS!
©COONER 2/7/2024

OR, LIKE THREE DAYS, AT THIS COMIC'S PACE.

SO, IS SAL GONNA PERFORM HERE?
WELL, I'M GOING TO ASK HIM TO. THING IS --

AS HIS CAREER HAS TAKEN OFF, HE'S BEEN PLAYING MUCH BIGGER VENUES ACROSS THE COUNTRY.

SO IT MAY TAKE SOME CONVINCING TO GET HIM TO PLAY -- YOU KNOW.
©COONER 2/14/2024

AT A ONE-HORSE GAY BAR LIKE THE LAVENDER LION?
AN INDEPENDENT QUEER-OWNED-AND-OPERATED ONE-HORSE GAY BAR, IF YOU DON'T MIND.

Strip #162

YEAH, I'D LOVE TO TALK SAL INTO PERFORMING HERE.
SO HOW ARE YOU GONNA CONVINCE HIM?

WELL, HE DOES HAVE A WEAKNESS THAT I COULD EXPLOIT.
OOH? WHAT'S THAT?

WELL, HE DOESN'T MENTION IT OFTEN, BUT HE KINDA HAS A THING FOR ... FOR ... WELL --
YEAH?

FOR TALL ... MUSCULAR ... AQUATIC ... MAMMALS --
OOOOH!!!
©COONER 2/21/2024

SO, I *SUSPECT* THAT SAL WOULD BE -- *INTRIGUED* BY YOUR *BOYFRIEND* --
AND WITH *THAT* IN MIND --

I WOULD LIKE TO INVITE *YOU* AND *OCEAN* TO DINNER WITH *ME* AND MY *HUSBAND* TONIGHT.
OH, *LANCE!* I'M SO GLAD YOU'VE *WARMED* UP TO OCEAN FINALLY!

EH -- *WARMING* UP. IT'S A *PROCESS.*
BUT YOU'RE *COMFORTABLE* PLANNING A *DINNER!*

WELL. *LATE-STAGE CAPITALISM* CAN MAKE US DO *CRAZY THINGS* SOMETIMES.
©COONER 2/28/2024

Strip #164

WELL, IN ANY CASE, WE ACCEPT YOUR DINNER INVITATION!
THANK YOU, PRIDE.

AND I'LL MAKE SURE HE WEARS SOMETHING REVEALING!
WELL, I GUESS THAT'S MOST OF HIS WARDROBE NOW --

HMMMM. I WONDER HOW OCEAN IS DOING AT HIS NEW JOB.
©COONER 3/6/2024

YES, YOU CAN CHANGE OUTFITS IN EL ALMACÉN!
SUPPLY CLOSET

WELL, HERE I AM! A JOB IS A JOB, AFTER ALL!
A TACO A DAY KEEPS THE ENNUI AWAY

THOUGH I'LL ADMIT, I NEVER THOUGHT I'D BE DRESSED AS A SIX-FOOT TACO.

MMM, MMMMM-- SIX FOOT TACO--

WELL *HEY* THERE, *STUD!* I SAW YOU FROM DOWN THE *BLOCK.*
HI THERE, *HAYLIE.* OH?
YOU CAN'T BEAT OUR MEAT TACOS

YOU'RE KIND OF *HARD* TO *MISS.* ALSO, NICE *DUDS.*
THANKS! THE SUIT *FIT,* SO I GOT THE *JOB.*

NICE. WELL, LET ME KNOW IF YOU NEED HELP *PEELING IT OFF* LATER.

I'D STILL LOVE TO SEE *YOUR* MEAT!
YOU CAN'T BEAT OUR MEAT TACOS
©COONER 3/20/2024

¡OCEAN, MI AMIGO! HOW IS IT GOING OUT HERE?
GETTING BY! HOW'S BUSINESS?
©COONER 3/27/2024

¡NO ME QUEJO!
IT'S A SLOW DAY BUT YOU'VE BROUGHT IN A FEW NEW CUSTOMERS.
HOORAY!

PERO BUENO, YOU'VE BEEN OUT HERE ALMOST AN HOUR--

I FIGURED THAT I'D BETTER BRING YOU A SIX-PACK OF TACOS.
BOSS, YOU KNOW THE WAY TO MY HEART!

SO, I NEED TO PICK UP SOME *EQUIPMENT* IN *GARDEN CITY.*
I'LL BE BACK IN A COUPLE OF *HOURS.*
©COONER 4/3/2024

YOU GONNA BE *OKAY* TIL I GET BACK?
I THINK SO, BOSS!

MUY BIEN. I WANT TO INTRODUCE YOU TO MY *ABUELA, ALMA ÁGUILA!*
SHE'LL BE *LA JEFA,* RUNNING THINGS UNTIL I GET BACK.

HELLO, MRS. *ÁGUILA!*
¡VIRGEN SANTÍSIMA, PEPE! I DIDN'T REALIZE YOU'D HIRED *KING KONG!*

BUENO, I'LL BE BACK AS SOON AS I CAN!
SI, PEPE CARIÑO, DRIVE CAREFULLY!

OCEAN, I WANT TO WELCOME YOU TO THE TACO HUT FAMILY!
THANK YOU, MRS. ÁGUILA! I'M GLAD TO BE HERE!

I NEED TO GET BACK TO THE KITCHEN, BUT PLEASE, CALL ME ABUELA!
AWW, WILL DO! AND IF YOU NEED HELP INSIDE, LET ME KNOW!

¡SI! IF I NEED THE REFRIGERATOR MOVED, I WILL HOLLER!

WHOAH!
HELLO THERE!
MMM TACOS
VICTORY Q-HIGH #42
42

HOLY CRAP, DUDE, YOU ARE STACKED!!
THANKS!
42

DID YOU EVER PLAY FOOTBALL AT QUEERTON HIGH?
HMMM, NO--
42

BUT I DID KISS A QUARTERBACK ONE TIME!
42

DAAAMN DUDE. DID YOU GET THIS BIG JUST EATING TACOS?!
WELL, I CAN POLISH OFF A COUPLE TACO TWELVE-PACKS PRETTY EASILY--

GUYS!! WE TOTALLY NEED TO LOAD UP ON THESE TACOS!!

#66
VICTORY
FIGHT
Q
Woo!
QUEERTON #1
QUEERTON HIGH
DIVISION CHAMPS
©COONER 4/24/2024

Strip #172

¡HOLA!
OPEN
WELL THEN.
I GUESS PEPE'S
TACO SUIT REALLY
WORKS.
MI TACO
SU TACO
©COONER 5/1/2024

CARLITOS, WE'RE RUNNING LOW ON TORTILLAS! ¡APÚRATE! MAKE AS MANY AS YOU CAN!
YES, ABUELA!

UGH, THE TORTILLA PRESS IS JAMMING UP AGAIN--

HEY, EVERYTHING GOING OKAY IN HERE? THE CROWD IS GETTING PRETTY THICK--
©COONER 5/8/2024

OH MY GOD--!
PTANG!

ABUELA! ABUELA! THE TORTILLA PRESS FINALLY BROKE!
¿¡QUE!? ¡AY, NO! WE HAVE SO MANY CUSTOMERS WAITING!

PEPE COULD FIX THIS, BUT HE WON'T BE BACK FOR HOURS--
ABUELA, WHAT CAN WE DO?
©COONER 5/15/2024

WE CAN-- AAH, AHH--

THWACK!

¡AY! WHAT CAN WE DO?
WELL, NOW, JUST A MOMENT--

THE LEVER JUST PRESSES THE PLATE DOWN ON THIS DOUGH BALL, RIGHT--?

≈SQUISH≈
©COONER 5/22/2024

¡AAAH, DIOS MIO! IT IS THE MOST PERFECT TORTILLA I'VE EVER SEEN!

Strip #176

AAAAHH! ABUELA, WE'RE ALMOST OUT OF SHELLS!

OH, DO NOT WORRY, CARIÑO! OCEAN IS ON THE JOB!
©COONER 5/29/2024

≷SQUISH≷
≷SQUISH≷
≷SQUISH≷

OCEAN, YOU ARE A GODSEND! THANK YOU FOR HELPING TODAY!
GLAD TO HELP!

HONESTLY IT WAS NICE TO GET A BREAK FROM STANDING OUT THERE WEARING THE TACO SUIT!
©COONER 6/12/2024

AY, CARIÑO, BUT YOU LOOK SO GOOD IN IT! YOU REMIND ME OF MY PEPE!
REALLY?

WELL-- IF PEPE HAD UNAS CHICHOTAS LIKE YOURS!

OH, MRS. AG-- I MEAN, ABUELA-- YOU'RE SO KIND!
I CAN SEE WHERE PEPE GETS HIS PERSONALITY FROM!

YOU KNOW, IT'S KIND OF FUNNY--

I NEVER REALIZED THAT PEPE WAS ADOPTED!
©COONER 6/19/2024

¡AY! PLEASE DO NOT TELL PEPE, I DO NOT THINK HE KNOWS!

SI, IT IS TRUE--
MY LATE HUSBAND ARTURO AND I RAISED PEPE AS OUR OWN--
©COONER 7/31/2024

IN THOSE EARLY DAYS, ARTURO RAN A RASPADOS CART TO SUPPORT US.
RASPADO

ONE DAY HE FOUND A SORPRESA IN HIS MORNING'S SHIPMENT OF FRESH ICE--

--¡UN OSITO POLAR BEBÉ!
...TO BE CONTINUED!

Strip #180

TRYING TO FIND WHERE THE BABY CAME FROM, *ARTURO* LEARNED THAT HIS *ICE SHIPMENT* HAD BEEN MIXED UP WITH ONE FROM A *NEARBY NIGHTCLUB.*

ARTURO RESOLVED THAT HE WOULD NOT HAND OVER THIS TESORITO TO SUCH A VIOLENT CARTEL!

AND SO WE FLED THE TERRITORY AND RAN TO CALIFURNIA, WHERE WE COULD RAISE YOUNG PEPE IN SAFETY AS OUR OWN HIJITO!

WOW! THAT IS ONE AMAZING STORY, ABUELA!
¡MUCHAS GRACIAS, OCEAN!

AND THE STRIP HAS FINALLY HAD ITS FIRST OFFICIAL FLASHBACK!
OH! MY PLEASURE!
©COONER 8/14/2024

¡SANTO CIELO! WHAT'S BEEN GOING ON HERE?
WE HAD A MASSIVE RUSH AND A SITUATION, BUT WE MANAGED, WITH OCEAN'S HELP!

¿AH, SÍ? SO HE REALLY IS MORE THAN THE SIMPLE FOOL HE SOMETIMES SEEMS TO BE?
©COONER 8/21/2024

YES! AND HE'S A MASSIVE MOUNTAIN OF MUSCLE--

WHAT'S THAT, CARLOS?
SIR!! I MEAN--HE PERFORMED VERY ADMIRABLY UNDER PRESSURE!!

OCEAN, *CARLOS* AND *ABUELA* TOLD ME WHAT YOU *DID* TODAY! I CAN'T THANK YOU *ENOUGH*.
NO *PROBLEM*, BOSS!

AND NOT *JUST* THE HELP IN THE KITCHEN--
--BUT BRINGING IN ALL THAT LOCAL *FOOTBALL BUSINESS*? STROKE OF *GENIUS*!
AAAH, WELL--
©COONER 8/28/2024

YOU'LL BE *PLEASED* TO KNOW WE'VE COME UP WITH A NEW *MENU* ITEM, EN TU HONOR!
REALLY??

TACO HUT PRESENTS
OFFICIAL OCEAN'S OAXACA TACOS!!!
* 3 full lbs of beef, chicken, or salmon
* Cheese, kelp, tomatoes, sour cream
* Squid ink salsa, mild or spicy
All the protein you need for a full day on the gridiron!

Strip #184

PEPE, I'M TOUCHED! I'VE NEVER HAD A TACO NAMED AFTER ME BEFORE!

IT'S RESPECT FOR YOU--
AND GOOD MARKETING FOR OUR NEW CUSTOMER BASE!
©COONER 9/4/2024

PERO TAMBIÉN, YOU DESERVE A MORE PRACTICAL SHOW OF THANKS--

MUNCH
MUNCH
MUNCH

OCEAN, YOU SAVED THE DAY, AND MAYBE MY JOB!
MAY-- MAY I THANK YOU?
WHAT? OF COURSE, IF YOU WANT!

THANK YOU.

©COONER 9/11/2024

YOU OKAY, CARLOS?
PLEASE, JUST LET ME STAY HERE FOUR MORE HOURS--

Strip #186

GRACIAS DE NUEVO FOR YOUR *HELP* TODAY, OCEAN--AFTER ALL THAT YOU MUST BE *EXHAUSTED!*
OH, *NO*, NOT REALLY!

ALL THOSE *TACOS* YOU MADE *RE-ENERGIZED* ME AND REALLY HIT THE *SPOT!*
©COONER 9/18/2024

YOU WANT ANOTHER *MEDIA DOCENA TACO* PACK?
I *MEAN*, I WOULDN'T SAY *NO*--

PERO BUENO, YOU'VE HAD A BUSY DAY, AND I'D SAY YOU'VE MORE THAN EARNED YOUR KEEP!

AFTER THAT RUSH, WE'RE GOING TO CLOSE A BIT EARLY-- YOU'RE FREE TO HEAD HOME NOW!
OH, THANK YOU!

WAIT-- CLOSE? ISN'T THE STORE OPEN 24 HOURS?
©COONER 10/2/2024

OH, WE'LL REOPEN AGAIN IN CINCO MINUTOS!

PHEW! IT SURE HAS BEEN A DAY!
HEY, I COULD GO TO PRIDE'S BAR FOR AN AFTER-WORK DRINK!
©COONER 10/9/2024

HMM. I DON'T FEEL LIKE WALKING ACROSS TOWN AGAIN--
BUT I DON'T FIT ON THE BUS ANYMORE--

IF ONLY I COULD FIND A DIFFERENT MODE OF TRANSPORTATION--
SOMETHING THAT'S MORE OPEN-AIR, AND MORE SPACIOUS--

PAW·DI·CAB

HEY THERE! CAN YOU TAKE ME TO THE LAVENDER LION CLUB?
YOWZA! I CAN, BUT I'D HAVE TO CHARGE YOU AS TWO ADULT PASSENGERS!

OH, NO PROBLEM!
I'M FLUSH AFTER MY DAY AT THE NEW JOB!

ALRIGHT! YOU ALL IN? LET'S GO!
PAW

HNNG!
PAW

97

Strip #190

UMM-- ARE YOU OKAY UP THERE?

:HUFF: DON'T WORRY, MISTER! I GOT THIS!
HMM. I MIGHT HAVE A BETTER IDEA--

PAW·DI·CAB

PAW·DI·CAB

NOW THERE'S SOMETHING YOU DON'T SEE EVERY DAY, CHAUNCEY.
WHAT'S THAT, EDGAR?
BUS STOP

A BIG, OVERMUSCLED OTTER CARRYING A PEDICAB.
BUS STOP

SORRY, THAT'S LITERALLY ALL I'VE GOT THIS TIME!
VERY LITERALLY!
BUS STOP

Strip #192

LANCCCE-- I LOVE YOUR ESSSTABLISHMENT SSSO MUCH!
CHAD, OCCCEAN--SSSO MANY SSSTUDS! I LOVESSS THEM ALL!!

THANK YOU, SANDY. I THINK YOU'VE HAD A FEW TOO MANY.
NONSSSENSSSE! I'M SSSOBER AS A CHURCH MOUSSSE!

EVEN SO. WE'RE GOING TO CALL A RIDE FOR YOU.
OH, HEY! LANCE!

I'VE GOT A PEDICAB READY RIGHT HERE!
PAW-DI-CAB
©COONER 11/6/2024

OCCCEAN! WE WERE JUSSST TALKING ABOUT YOU, HANDSSSSOME BOY!

MY STRONG, TRUSSSTWORTHY SSSTEED HASSS ARRIVED WITH MY SSSURREY!

OH, PILLOWSSS? DON'T MIND IF I DO!

--IS HE OKAY?
A FIVE MARTINI LUNCH. VERY SMALL LIVER.

WHAT DO I OWE YOU, GOOD SIR?

WELL, LET ME GIVE YOU A TIP, AT LEAST!
DUDE, YOU CARRIED ME! AND LED ME TO ANOTHER FARE!

AND HERE, I'LL PAY FOR THE SNAKE'S RIDE HOME, TOO!
THANKS!

I HOPE SO. THIS HAS BEEN HAPPENING A LOT LATELY.
UMM--IS HE ALRIGHT IN THERE?

THAT WAS A GENEROUS TIP, OCEAN.
YEAH! I HAD A GREAT DAY, SO WHY NOT?!

SOO--GOOD SHIFT AT THE NEW JOB?
OH, FOR SURE! A REALLY GOOD TIME!

NOTHING--BAD HAPPENED?
NOPE! I EVEN GOT A BONUS!

OH, BLESSED BE!!!

WELL, THAT IS GREAT NEWS, OCEAN. I'M VERY HAPPY FOR YOU.
GOSH, THANKS, LANCE! I APPRECIATE THAT!

NOW THEN, ABOUT DINNER TONIGHT--
DINNER?

OH, YES! I'M TAKING YOU TO CHEZ RONGEUR.
OH?

DINNER? TONIGHT?

YES. TO BE QUITE BLUNT--
--I REQUIRE THE PRESENCE OF A TALL, MUSCULAR AQUATIC MAMMAL.*
OH--
*--AS DISCUSSED IN STRIP #162!

IT WILL BE FUN! THE RESTAURANT IS VERY ROMANTIC.

GOSH, UMM, LANCE--I DON'T KNOW WHAT TO SAY--
HMM.

I'M TORN. ON THE ONE HAND, THIS IS A NICE PLACE, SO PLEASE TRY TO DRESS UP A LITTLE.

BUT ALSO, MAKE SURE YOU WEAR SOMETHING A BIT REVEALING!
I'LL SEE YOU THERE, HON!

OH, GOSH. LANCE IS A NICE GUY--
BUT HE'S NOT REALLY MY TYPE, Y'KNOW?

BUT ALSO, HE'S PRIDE'S BOSS--
IF I REFUSE, COULD IT COST HIM HIS JOB?

OH, WHAT WOULD MARCIA BRADY DO?!

OCEAN, HUNNY! HOW WAS YOUR DAY?

OOF. HONESTLY, I THINK I NEED A STIFF DRINK.
AWW. DON'T WORRY, I HAVE JUST THE THING.

©COONER 1/22/2025

HAPPY 200TH STRIP!

HEY, PRIDE, WHAT'S YOUR STRONGEST DRINK?
OH! THAT WOULD BE MY OPA!-SOM!

IT'S OUZO, SHAKEN WITH MY SECRET BLEND OF LIQUORS AND MIXERS!
©COONER 1/29/2025

:GULP:
CAREFUL! ONE OF THOSE WILL KNOCK YOU ON YOUR ASS INSTANTLY!

BUT I DON'T FEEL ANYTHING.
HMM. YOU DO HAVE A LOT OF EXTRA BODY MASS NOW.

;GULP;

ANOTHER PLEASE!

;GULP;

I'M NOT GETTING DRUNK!!
©COONER 2/5/2025

⌇GULP⌇

ANOTHER PLEASE!

⌇GULP⌇
©COONER 2/12/2025

ANOTHER PLEASE!
OCEAN, WHAT'S ON YOUR *MIND?*

PRIDE, I GOTTA ASK YOU SOMETHING.
SURE!

LANCE-- UH-- JUST ASKED ME TO DINNER.
©COONER 2/19/2025

OH, YEAH! IF YOU CAN GO, IT'LL BE A BIG HELP!
YOU ALREADY KNOW?!

YEAH! IT SOUNDS PRETTY ROMANTIC, DOESN'T IT?
--HE KNOWS!!

HUNNY, YOU KNOW HOW MUCH I LOVE YOU!
YES, OF COURSE!

AND I WOULD DO ANYTHING FOR YOU!
I KNOW!

SO, SINCE THIS MEANS THAT MUCH TO YOU--
©COONER 8/20/2025

I WILL SLEEP WITH LANCE FOR YOU!!
WHAT?!

IF IT WILL SAVE YOUR JOB, I'LL SLEEP WITH LANCE!!
WHAT ARE YOU TALKING ABOUT?!

IT'S THE REASON LANCE INVITED ME TO DINNER!
OCEAN! HE INVITED US TO DINNER!
DID YOU SEE ANY OF MY TEXTS TODAY?

OH! MY PHONE!
©COONER 8/27/2025

≠tap≠
≠tap≠

≠scroll≠
≠scroll≠

OH--
OKAY--

YEAH, OKAY -- I TOTALLY MISREAD THE SITUATION!
YA THINK?!
©COONER 9/3/2025

SO THIS IS A DOUBLE-DATE SORTA THING?
YEAH, KINDA--

LANCE WANTS TO ASK HIS HUSBAND SAL TO COME DO A NIGHTCLUB ACT.
BRING THE LAVENDER LION A LITTLE EXTRA BUSINESS.

SAL IS A BIG FAN OF TALL, MUSCULAR, AQUATIC MAMMALS.
LANCE THOUGHT HAVING ONE THERE MIGHT PUT HIM IN AN AGREEABLE FRAME OF MIND.

LANCE THOUGHT OF ME?!
SHOCKING, I KNOW!
©COONER 9/10/2025

SO -- YOUR JOB'S NOT IN DANGER?
OH, NO NO NO, NOTHING LIKE THAT!

YOUR TASK IS JUST TO BE YOUR NEW, BIG, MUSCULAR --
≷twitch≷

UH -- SEXY -- SELF --
©COONER 9/17/2025

≷BOUNCE≷
≷BOUNCE≷

HEY--WAIT A MINUTE. THIS IS WHERE WE ARE AGAIN?!
HMM?

SO NOT JUST YOU, BUT NOW YOUR BOSS, TREATING ME LIKE A SLAB OF MEAT TO PUT ON DISPLAY?
UHH--

©COONER 9/24/2025

OH GOSH, THAT'S STILL PRETTY HOT--
RIGHT?!

THAT JUST LEAVES ONE QUESTION, THEN--
WHAT'S THAT?

WHY DOESN'T LANCE WANT ME?!

JUST KIDDING, HUNNY!
OH, YOU!
©COONER 10/1/2025

STILL, I'M SORRY I MISSED THAT CALL.
WELL, IT SURE SOUNDS LIKE YOU HAD A REALLY BUSY DAY!

I DID!
AND I ATE A LOT OF TACOS!

≳RUMBLE≲

SPEAKING OF -- WHEN'S THIS DINNER?
IN JUST A COUPLE HOURS, SILLY!
©COONER 10/8/2025

YOU GUYS READY FOR TONIGHT'S DINNER?
ALMOST! I'M GONNA TAKE OFF A BIT EARLY TO FIND OCEAN SOMETHING NICE TO WEAR, IS THAT OKAY?

OF COURSE! GOOD LUCK!
THANKS!
AND THANKS FOR THE DINNER INVITE!

AND LANCE -- JUST SO YOU KNOW --
I ABSOLUTELY, POSITIVELY, TOTALLY DID NOT THINK YOU WERE TRYING TO SLEEP WITH ME!

©COONER 10/15/2025

HEY, CHAD, I HAVE TO -- CHAD?!
:GROAN:

ARE YOU OKAY?
OH! YEAH!

I'M JUST, UH, A LITTLE TIRED OUT TODAY.
HAYLIE HAD ME UP PRETTY LATE LAST NIGHT -- KNOW WHAT I MEAN?

GOT IT, CHAD. UMMM-- GOOD FOR YOU!
WINK, WINK, EH?
©COONER 10/22/2025

ANYWAY, I NEED TO LEAVE A BIT EARLY. CAN YOU KEEP AN EYE ON THE BAR?
SURE THING, BUDDY!

HAVE A FUN EVENING!
WILL DO! YOU TOO, CHAD!

THAT WAS CLOSE! DID HE SEE ME?
I DON'T THINK SO, BABE!
©COONER 10/29/2025

THERE'S A CLOTHES SHOP A FEW BLOCKS AWAY --
GOSH, I'M SO SORRY, PRIDE.

FOR WHAT?
I'VE CAUSED SO MANY COMPLICATIONS -- AND SO MANY MISUNDERSTANDINGS --I'VE UPENDED OUR LIVES COMPLETELY!

OCEAN! DON'T BE SILLY. YOU'RE STILL MY TRUE LOVE AND I'M HAPPY TO BE WITH YOU!
AWWW!
©COONER 11/05/2025

PLUS-- Y'KNOW--YOU'RE, LIKE, INCREDIBLY HOT NOW--
HEEHEE. TRUE.

OKAY. *C'MON*, PRIDE.
HMM?

GO AHEAD. YOU *KNOW* YOU WANNA.
YOU MEAN--?

YUP. *GO* FOR IT.
IF YOU *INSIST*--

LOVE YOU, HUNNY!
LUFF OO TOO!
©COONER 11/12/2025

...but that's not all!

Pride and Ocean aren't finished yet! Ocean needs to find some nice clothes, and their dinner with Lance's husband Sal is just around the corner! And there are still those shadowy agents from Genet•IX Labs to worry about! Follow along as Ocean continues to get used to his new size and Pride tries to keep up with him. New strips are posted weekly(ish) at any of these locations online:

Official web site: https://mybiggerboyfriend.com

Telegram channel: https://t.me/mybiggerboyfriend

On my Bluesky account: https://bsky.app/profile/cooner.art

On my Mastodon account: https://meow.social/@cooner

On my FurAffinity page: http://www.furaffinity.net/user/cooner

Or, you can join our community on Patreon, support the comic with a few dollars a month, see strips two weeks early, and find some additional perks as well!

https://www.patreon.com/cooner

Addendum: Holiday Ornaments!

During the holiday season of 2022, I posted these two *My Bigger Boyfriend* holiday ornaments of Pride and Ocean for fans to print and cut out. Feel free to cut them out yourself! (Except maybe make a photocopy of those pages and cut THOSE out instead … You paid good money for this book!)

Pride Possum 2022 Holiday Ornament!

1. Print this comic onto a sheet of heavy paper. BONUS: Check your printer settings first to make the ornament print at the size you want!

2. Carefully cut out along the dotted black line. Do not use pinking shears. Unless you want to. You do you!

3. Punch a hole where the blue dot is. You can use a paper punch, an awl, the tip of a pencil ... just be careful not to puncture your hand too!

4. Use an ornament hook, a length of string, or a twisted paper clip through the hole to hang ornament on your tree.

5. Sit back, bask in the glow, and enjoy the holiday season!

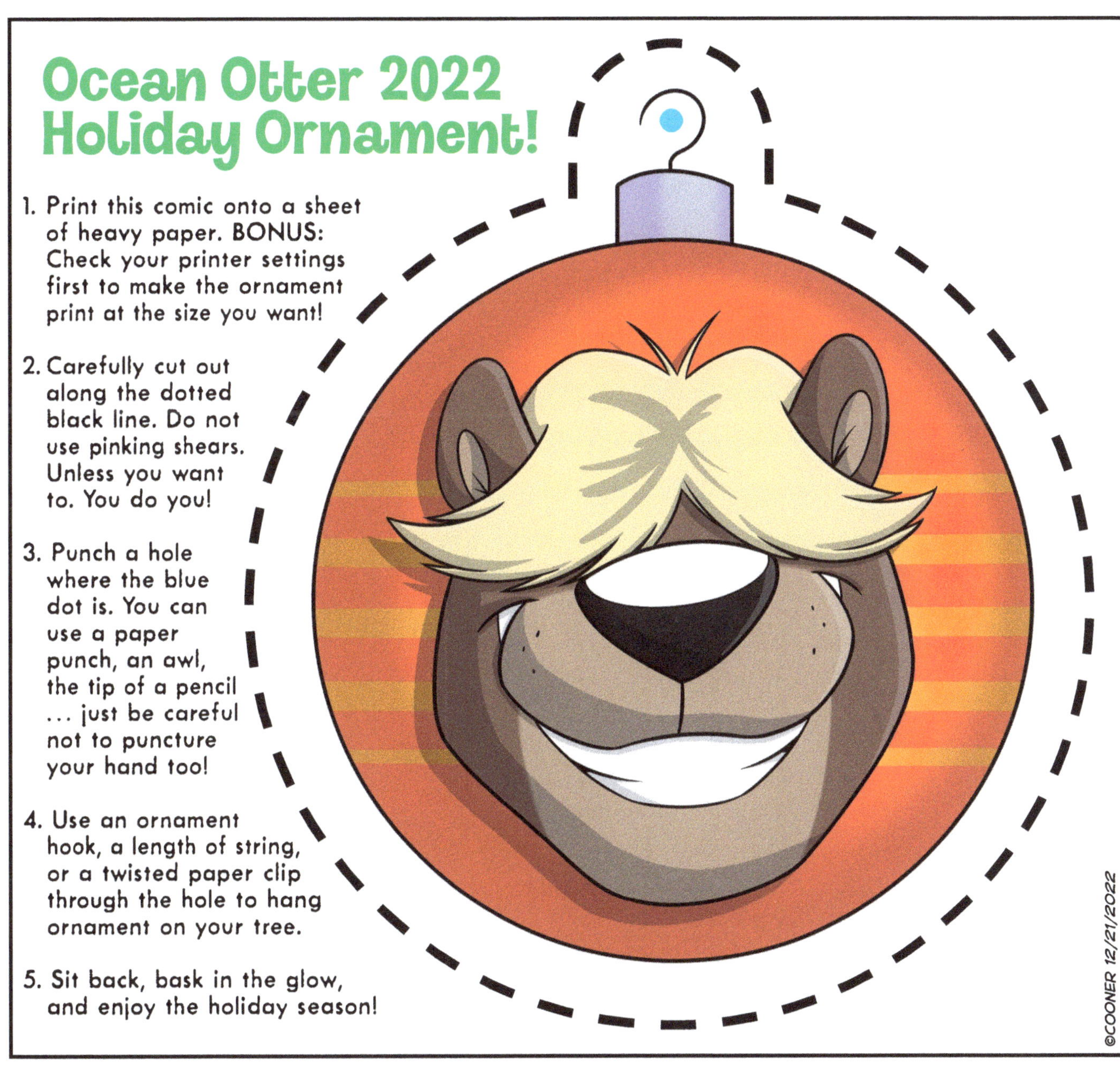

Ocean Otter 2022 Holiday Ornament!

1. Print this comic onto a sheet of heavy paper. BONUS: Check your printer settings first to make the ornament print at the size you want!

2. Carefully cut out along the dotted black line. Do not use pinking shears. Unless you want to. You do you!

3. Punch a hole where the blue dot is. You can use a paper punch, an awl, the tip of a pencil ... just be careful not to puncture your hand too!

4. Use an ornament hook, a length of string, or a twisted paper clip through the hole to hang ornament on your tree.

5. Sit back, bask in the glow, and enjoy the holiday season!

Addendum: Fan Art!

Ever since first publishing *My Bigger Boyfriend*, I've been thrilled and honored to receive artwork of Pride and Ocean from so many other artists and fans of the strip! Here's a selection of just a few of the favorites I've seen … though of course I love and appreciate every one!

Art by Steakkums • bsky.app/profile/steakkums.bsky.social

Art by Freckles • linktr.ee/elfreckles

GROW

Art by Overkelion • www.furaffinity.net/user/overkelion
Wolf character belongs to Jim55

Art by Narf Raccoon • bsky.app/profile/narfraccoon.bsky.social

That's another wrap!

Thanks again for reading … and hopefully see you in a couple years with *My Bigger Boyfriend Volume Three!* In the meantime, again, you can continue to follow the strip, posted Wednesdays online at any of these locations.

Official web site: https://mybiggerboyfriend.com

Telegram channel: https://t.me/mybiggerboyfriend

On my Bluesky account: https://bsky.app/profile/cooner.art

On my Mastodon account: https://meow.social/@cooner

On my FurAffinity page: http://www.furaffinity.net/user/cooner

Or, you can join our community on Patreon, support the comic with a few dollars a month, see strips two weeks early, and find some additional perks as well!

https://www.patreon.com/cooner